THIS BOOK BELONGS TO

D0812890

....

I CELEBRATED WORLD BOOK DAY 20 WITH
THIS BRILLIANT GIFT FROM MY LOCAL BOOKSELLER,
PENGUIN RANDOM HOUSE CHILDREN'S UK
AND JACQUELINE WILSON!

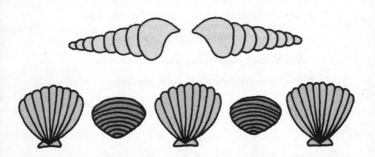

This book has been specially written and
published to celebrate 20 years of
World Book Day. For further information, visit
www.worldbookday.com

World Book Day in the UK and Ireland
is made possible by generous sponsorship
from National Book Tokens, participating
publishers, authors, illustrators and
booksellers. Booksellers who accept the
£1* World Book Day Book Token bear
the full cost of redeeming it.

World Book Day, World Book Night and
Quick Reads are annual initiatives designed
to encourage everyone in the UK and Ireland –
whatever your age – to read more and discover
the joy of books and reading for pleasure.

World Book Night is a celebration of books and
reading for adults and teens on 23 April, which
sees book gifting and celebrations in thousands
of communities around the country:
www.worldbooknight.org

Quick Reads provides brilliant short new
books by bestselling authors to engage
adults in reading:
www.quickreads.org.uk

*€1.50 in Ireland

CORGI BOOKS

UK | USA | Canada | Ireland | Australia
India | New Zealand | South Africa

Corgi Books is part of the Penguin Random House group of companies
whose addresses can be found at global.penguinrandomhouse.com.

www.penguin.co.uk   www.puffin.co.uk   www.ladybird.co.uk

First published 2017

001

Set in 10.25/17pt New Century Schoolbook by Becky Chilcott
Printed in Great Britain by Clays Ltd, St Ives plc

A CIP catalogue record for this book is available from the British Library

ISBN: 978–0–552–57622–2

All correspondence to:
Corgi Books
Penguin Random House Children's
80 Strand, London WC2R 0RL

Jacqueline Wilson

Butterfly

ILLUSTRATED BY
NICK SHARRATT

Beach

CORGI BOOKS

I'M SELMA JOHNSON. If you go to my school you'll have heard of me. I was the worst girl in the whole of the Infants. I got suspended three times, even though I was just a little kid.

I was even worse when I went up into Year Three. Everyone was scared of me, even the really big tough boys in Year Six. Well, Year Five. OK, they might have been in Year Four, but they were still really horrible to everyone else. I showed them, though. I was a champion fighter – *biff, bang, wallop* – using my fists.

I said all sorts of stuff too. Sometimes I didn't even need to say anything, I just *looked*, frowning so that my eyebrows almost met and my eyes went  all squinty and mean. My look was famous. Even the teachers shuddered when I gave them my look. Except Miss Lovejoy. *She's* famous for being a fierce old bag, almost as fierce as me.

Only I'm not fierce any more. I'm not mean or mouthy and I don't even nick stuff. I haven't been in a fight for ages and ages. It's all because of Tina. You know, Tina Maynard. Do you know her too? She's one of the triplets.

They're identical, Phil and Maddie and Tina. Three sisters with short fair hair and big blue eyes. To be absolutely truthful, I still sometimes get Phil and Maddie muddled up.

I always know which one's Tina. So does everyone. It's easy-peasy picking her out because she's half the size of her sisters. Well, maybe a bit more than half. But she only comes up to their shoulders, honest. It's because she was born with a funny heart and she was very ill when she was small. Smaller than she is now, I mean. She's still a little squirt. She's by far the littlest in our class. I'm the biggest.

I think I liked her right from the start, when Miss Lovejoy made us sit together right at the front of the class. Maybe I just envied her. She was the sort of girl I'd always secretly wanted to be. Little, cute, pretty. Everyone liked her and made a fuss of her, especially her sisters. When their mum picked the triplets up from school at the end of the day, she always smiled at them and asked them all sorts of stuff. She often picked Tina up and gave her a special hug, as if she was still a little baby. It made me feel all hot and aching and envious.

So I started being mean to her. It was easy-peasy because she was such a little wuss. I kicked her under the table and jogged her arm when she was drawing. She was soooo good at drawing, whereas I can't draw for toffee. Once I scribbled all over her special butterfly picture. It felt good when I was doing it, but then, seeing the black scrubby mess on the page and knowing I'd ruined it, I felt sick.

I couldn't stop being mean to her, though. I liked seeing her funny little face screw up because she was trying not to cry. It meant I was top dog – big, powerful, menacing Selma. She was just silly little squirt Tina, and I could always get the better of her.

One day Tina brought this teeny little china dolly into school in secret, and I snatched it off her and pretended I'd flushed it down the toilet. I was going to, but that would have been *too* mean. And I wanted the dolly for myself. My horrible little brother Sam had just got hold of my old Princess Elsa doll and stamped on her. I asked Mum for another one, but she said I was too old for flipping dolls and to quit bothering her because I was doing her head in.

I loved Tina's little china dolly. I could keep her tucked safe in my hand so Sam couldn't see her. I'd go to sleep holding her, though sometimes I lay awake worrying that Tina didn't have anything to hold any more.

But she's *my* dolly now. Tina said I could have her – because we're not worst enemies any more, we're best friends! Our teacher, Miss Lovejoy, picked us to make a butterfly garden out of an old patch of earth at the end of the playground. I did nearly all of it myself, digging and digging and digging.

Tina knew which flowers we needed, and we planted them all, and by the time school broke up the butterflies had started coming. Not heaps and heaps – Miss Lovejoy says it will take time – but we've seen some cabbage whites and a brimstone and quite a few red admirals. They're all types of butterfly. Tina's drawn a picture of each one in this Butterfly Diary we're keeping.

Miss Lovejoy has given us special permission to come into school during the holidays so we can look out for more butterflies in our garden. Not the whole class. Not even Phil and Maddie. Just Tina and me. Like I said, we're best friends now.

I've never actually had a proper best friend before. I've sometimes made kids *say* they were my friends, but that's just because they knew I'd wallop them if they didn't. But Tina is a real friend, truly. I've been to tea at her house heaps. She's been to my flat too. Once.

I didn't really like it, particularly when my stepdad, Jason, started having a go at me in front of her. Tina's sooo lucky having a proper dad who never gets ratty with her. He's ever so kind and funny. I've met her mum too, and she's OK, sort of, but her dad is magic. I once called him Dad by mistake, and then blushed and said sorry, but he laughed and said I could call him Dad any time. I don't see my real dad. I'm supposed to call Jason Dad but I'd never, ever do that. I can't stick him, and he can't stick me. I love my mum, but sometimes I can't help wish-wish-wishing I was part of Tina's family.

But guess what! I'm going on holiday with them. I am, truly – this Saturday. Tomorrow! We're going to the seaside, staying in a caravan! Tina's dad invited me.

I'd been dreading Tina going away on holiday.

'Cheer up, chickie!' Tina's dad said to me when I was round at their house for tea yesterday. 'Why are you looking all mopey?'

'Because I'm going to miss Tina so,' I said.

'And I'll miss you too, Selma!' said Tina, giving me a hug.

'But you've still got Phil and Maddie to play with. I haven't got anyone,' I moaned.

'You've got Sam,' said Tina's mum, though she didn't sound convinced.

She once invited my mum round to tea, so Sam and my baby brother, Joel, had to come too. Joel was OK. He just slept, even though he had a stinky nappy. But Sam kept switching their telly on and off, on and off, until the batteries stopped working. Tina's mum found him a picture book to look at but he ripped out all the pages. Then, when he went upstairs for a wee, he discovered the triplets' hamsters Nibbles and Speedy and Cheesepuff, and he scooped them out of their cage for a cuddle.

They ran off, and it took hours to find them again.

I rolled my eyes at the very thought of playing with Sam.

'Tell you what!' Tina's dad said suddenly. 'Why don't you come on holiday with us?'

They all looked startled, especially Tina's mum.

'Well, that's a lovely idea,' she said, 'but it's far too last minute. We're going on Saturday. We can't get it all sorted out in two days.'

'What's the problem? There's a bunk going spare in the kids' room in the caravan. There'll be room in the minivan. Sorted! It'll be fun, won't it?'

'Oh yes!' said Tina, and she gave her dad a hug, and then me a hug, and then went whirling around the room doing a happy dance.

Tina's mum didn't look very happy about the idea. Phil and Maddie seemed a bit put out too.

'Well, if Tina's having Selma, can my friend Neera come?' Phil asked.

'And I want my friend Harry,' said Maddie. 'It's only fair if Tina gets to have *her* friend.'

'Not this time, girls. You know we've only got one spare bunk bed,' said Dad.

'And it's Selma's!' Tina cried, and she seized my hands and made me join in her crazy dance. 'I'm so happy, happy, happy!' she sang.

I was so happy, happy, happy too. I couldn't wait to tell Mum. Tina's dad drove me home and came in with me to make sure it was all right.

'I'm going on holiday with Tina and her family!' I yelled the minute I got in the front door.

'Is that OK with you?' Tina's dad asked Mum. 'I know it's short notice, but it just suddenly seemed a good plan, and the kids are over the moon about it.'

Mum and Jason were watching some comedy quiz show on the telly, while Sam sat on the floor in just a T-shirt, gnawing on a soggy pizza crust, and Joel lay on a cushion, sucking on his bottle.

'That's nice,' Mum said absent-mindedly, watching the screen.

'Where you going then?' Jason asked.

'Bracing Beach in Norfolk. We've hired the same caravan as last year,' said Tina's dad.

'So you'll be packing your macs and wellies then,' said Jason, sneering. 'We're going to Paris, taking the kids to Disneyland.'

'Yay!' Sam yelled. 'Disneyland!'

'You never mentioned it before!' I said.

'Keeping it a surprise, wasn't I?' Jason said. 'We're off this Saturday, as a matter of fact.'

I looked at him, sure that he was bluffing. We never, ever went on holiday. I looked at Mum. She looked amazed, as if this trip was news to her too.

'Oh well, I've always wanted to go to Disneyland myself,' she said.

So had I! Oh, so much!

'It's a shame Selma can't go off to this beach place, wherever it is,' said Jason. 'Unless you'd *sooner* stay in a little caravan on the coast,

Selma . . . It's up to you. Disneyland, and all the rides and parades and fireworks – or the caravan?'

I shuffled from one foot to the other. He *was* bluffing. He'd been moaning on about being skint only that morning. He was just winding me up so I'd miss out on going on holiday with Tina.

I thought about it. Suppose they really *were* going to Disneyland . . . Who did I like best? Mickey and Minnie Mouse and Donald Duck and Pluto and all those fairy princesses – or Tina? To be honest, it was a bit of a struggle deciding. But Mickey Mouse and his pals weren't *real* friends. Tina was my best friend ever, my first and only best friend.

'I'd sooner go on holiday with Tina in the caravan,' I said.

Jason's face! I felt a real thrill then.

 Tina's dad looked worried. 'Oh, Selma, you can't miss out on a chance of going to Disneyland,' he said.

'Well, she just has,' said Jason curtly. 'So
be it.'

He didn't speak to me after that –
not on Thursday evening or on
Friday morning. As if I cared!
Mum was mad at me too, saying
I'd hurt his feelings and I was nasty and un-
grateful, and anyway, they'd have a much
better time without me at Disneyland.

I *did* care that she said that. She came
and found me crying in my room.

'Serves you right,' she said, but she must
have felt sorry, because while Jason was
seeing his mates at the Albert on Friday
lunch time, Mum slipped down to the shops.
She came back with two parcels – a big one
from Primark with a new T-shirt and pair of
shorts and swimming costume for me, and a
little one from BlingPhone.

I opened this one with trembling fingers.
It was a pink mobile phone covered in sparkly
pink gems.

'Oh, Mum!' I said.

I'd been wanting my own mobile for ages and ages, but she always said I should quit nagging her and I wasn't old enough anyway.

'Is it really mine?' I whispered.

'Of course it's yours. It's got twenty quid on it too. You can take holiday selfies, eh? I bet them triplets haven't got mobiles,' said Mum.

'But I thought Jason said we were skint,' I said.

'Well, it's what credit cards are for, isn't it?' said Mum. 'Are you pleased?'

'You bet,' I said, and I gave her a hug.

For a minute I wished I wasn't going away with Tina after all. I wanted to stick with Mum and be part of my own family, especially if we were going to Disneyland – though I didn't think that was likely. When Mum asked Jason about it straight out, he'd told her to shut up about it.

They certainly didn't get up early on Saturday morning to drive anywhere. They hadn't even done any packing. I'd packed my bag. I didn't have a proper case, but I stowed everything neatly in a checked plastic bag. I wrapped the baby doll Tina had given me in one of my socks and shoved her right down to the bottom. I wore my new T-shirt and shorts and put my sparkly pink mobile in my pocket.

Tina's dad said they'd pick me up at nine o'clock. I was ready and waiting at seven. Sam woke up too, and I made us bowls of cornflakes. I let him sprinkle on extra sugar – I even felt fond of him in a weird kind of way.

'Do you think you're really going to Disneyland?' I asked him.

'Disneyland, Disneyland, Disneyland,' he said, stirring his cornflakes round and round. He didn't know either.

I was worried that, if they really were going, they might miss their plane or train. I wanted to go and wake Mum, but I hated going into her bedroom because it was Jason's room too. I made Sam go instead because he can get away with murder.

He didn't come back for a while.

'I had a big cuddle with Mum and Dad,' he said when he emerged at last.

'Baby!' I said scornfully, though I wished I was little and cute enough for cuddles too. 'So did you ask Jason about Disneyland?'

'Disneyland, Disneyland—'

'OK, don't start that again! Are you going?' I interrupted.

'Dad just said, "Pipe down, son – you'll wake Joel and he was bawling half the night and I need a kip,"' said Sam.

So they almost definitely weren't going. Jason was a big fat liar. But *I* was going on holiday. I waited and waited, peering down out of the window, on the lookout for Tina's dad's van. At long last, at ten past nine, it drove up in front of Turner block.

'Here they are! I'm off!' I shouted, grabbing my bag.

'Wait a tick, lovey!' Mum shuffled out of

the bedroom in her nightie, her hair all over the place. 'Give us a hug.' She lowered her voice. 'You got your phone? You do realize what a lucky girl you are!'

'You bet I do, Mum,' I said.

I got a hug from her. I even got a hug from Sam. If you think I got a hug from Jason, you must be barking mad.

I ran all the way down the stairs. I hate going in that smelly lift and I couldn't risk one of the gang boys nicking my new pink mobile for a girlfriend. I was so out of breath when I got to the van, I couldn't even say hello, but I bobbed up and down excitedly instead.

'Hey, Selma! All set? Hop in the back with the girls,' said Tina's dad. 'I'll pop your bag in the boot for you.'

Phil and Maddie sat together. I got to sit with Tina. She grinned at me, giving my hand a big squeeze.

'Guess what!' I said as soon as I could speak. 'I've got a mobile!' I produced it proudly from my shorts pocket.

'Oh, wow!' said Tina.

'Mum, Selma's got her own mobile!' said Phil.

'Why aren't we allowed mobiles yet?' Maddie asked.

'Because I don't think you're old enough,' said Tina's mum stiffly.

'Mum, just look at Selma's mobile! It's all pink and sparkly!' said Tina.

'Very pretty,' said Tina's mum, but she sounded as if she meant the exact opposite. Perhaps she was jealous. She had a very ordinary metal phone that wasn't even top of the range.

'Come here, Tina,' I said, putting my arm round her and holding out my right hand, getting my phone at the right angle. 'Smile!'

Tina grinned and I clicked, and there was my very first selfie! I took lots and lots on the journey. We smiled and smiled, and then we pulled silly faces and shrieked with laughter when we saw the photos.

'Can I have a turn taking one?' Tina begged.

I wanted to take all the photos myself – it was *my* mobile, after all – but Tina was my best friend for ever.

'OK,' I said light-heartedly, and handed my phone over.

Tina wasn't anywhere near as good at taking photos as me. For a start her arm wasn't long enough for selfies, not if she wanted to include me in them too. And she was so excited she couldn't keep her hand still, so we came out all weird and blurry. But I didn't complain. You shouldn't boss your best friend around all the time, even though you might want to.

'Can I have a turn, Selma?' Phil asked.

'And me? Please let me,' Maddie said.

You should share with your best friend, but sometimes you have to draw the line at your best friend's *sisters*.

I ignored them, so Tina did too. They begged harder.

'Stop going on at me,' I snapped.

'But why won't you let us have a go?' asked Phil.

'It's my turn now,' said Maddie, and she tried to snatch the mobile off Tina.

'Stop it!' I said, and I snatched it back.

Maddie gave a little gasp.

'Selma!' said Tina's mum.

'I didn't do anything!' I said. Well, I might have accidentally on purpose given her the tiniest shove, but I didn't *hurt* her.

'Yes you did,' said Phil. 'Come on now, Selma, don't be so mean. You've let Tina take heaps of photos.'

'But Tina's my best friend,' I said.

'Phil and Maddie are your friends too,' said Tina's mum.

'No they're not,' I muttered in a very tiny voice so they couldn't quite hear.

'Let's give the photos a rest and have a sing-song,' said Tina's dad. 'Me first. Right, Selma, prepare to be amazed. The King of Rock, Elvis himself, has been reincarnated in Yours Truly. Imagine me with the quiff, the sideways smile, the wiggly hips, the blue suede shoes.'

He started singing all these songs about hound dogs and hotels and jailhouses and tender love. The triplets groaned but they sang along too, and even Tina's mum joined in.

'Come on, Selma, sing up,' said Tina's dad.

But I didn't know any of the words. We didn't sing much at home. I sat clutching my mobile, fingering the little pink beads. I wanted to take more selfies but I managed to stop myself. Then Tina's dad started singing a song about going on a summer holiday. I didn't know that one either, but he sang it three times, and by then I knew the tune and most of the words. We sang it and sang it and sang it, and I felt a lot better.

It was a long way to Bracing Beach, so we had lunch in a motorway café on the way. There was so much food I didn't know what to choose. I wondered about simply copying Tina, but she's got the appetite of a mouse. She just wanted half a tuna wrap and an orange juice. I didn't want the other half so her mum had it instead. Phil and Maddie had ham sandwiches and shared a packet of crisps. All this sharing was a bit unnerving!

'Well, it's the holidays, so I'm not sharing with anyone,' said Tina's dad. 'I'm going to have a huge all-day breakfast – bacon and egg and sausage and tomato and baked beans and mushrooms – and a portion of chips, yum yum. Why don't you be wicked too, Selma? What's your favourite food?'

'Chips,' I said.

'Then you have a great big plateful of chips, sweetheart. And what would you like to go with them?'

'Could I have tomato sauce, please?' I asked.

Phil and Maddie rolled their eyes. 'Dad

means, do you want chicken and chips, or sausage and chips, or fish and chips,' said Phil.

'Well, I don't,' I said, though I did actually like the sound of all those. 'I'd just like tomato sauce.'

'Your wish is my command, O Selma,' said Tina's dad, and he ordered a double portion of chips for me and took three sachets of tomato sauce from the stand.

I really, *really* love Tina's dad.

Phil and Maddie and even Tina started it's-not-fairing because they wanted a plate of chips too.

'Don't be silly, girls. You know you're only allowed chips as a special treat,' said their mum, glaring at their dad.

I was astonished. At home we had chips every single day. It's a wonder my feet didn't wear a groove down the stairs, past Blake block and Constable block to the chippie on the Parade.

I took a photo of my huge plate of chips with a big red circle of sauce, and then started shoving them into my mouth with my fingers. Tina's mum raised her eyebrows, so I sighed and used my fork, though they didn't taste quite so good that way. When she went to get two coffees, I quickly offered Tina a handful of chips. Phil and Maddie looked daggers. It was such fun winding them up.

Tina's dad shook his head at me, but he didn't get cross. Why, why, why couldn't my mum have found herself a bloke like him? Why did she have to lumber herself with Jason? Miss Lovejoy says there are some things we won't understand until we get older. I'm never going to understand what Mum sees in Jason even if I live to be a hundred.

The second part of the journey got a bit hot and boring. And I felt a bit queasy too, if I'm honest. I kept wondering if I should say anything or ask them to stop the van. I knew Tina's mum would be FURIOUS if I threw up. So I leaned back and shut my eyes and tried very, very hard not to be sick.

'Is she asleep?' I heard Tina's dad ask quietly.

'Yes – nodded right off,' said Tina's mum. She was whispering, but I could still hear her. 'Honestly, I'm not sure this is a good idea after all. This week's going to seem like a lifetime!'

'She's a nice little kid really,' said Tina's dad.

Tina's mum didn't reply.

Perhaps I really *did* fall asleep, because the next thing I knew Tina was clutching my hand and gently shaking me.

'We're here, Selma! We're here at Bracing Beach!'

It felt wonderful getting out of the hot, stuffy van and breathing in fresh sea air. We were up on the cliffs, parked beside the caravan site. We could see down to the cove and the sand and the sea. There didn't seem to be much else here. No pier, no amusement arcades, just a beach shop with buckets and spades and footballs and lilos, a little food shop called Camper's Cuisine, and an ice-cream van.

'Isn't it the loveliest place in the whole world?' said Tina.

'Yeah, it's fantastic,' I said uncertainly. It was so . . . empty.

Tina's family all seemed to love it. As soon as they'd got the suitcases stowed in the caravan they all ran down the zigzag steps to the beach. Even Tina's mum kicked off her espadrilles and went running towards the sea. Tina's dad took off his trainers and had a very splashy paddle. Phil and Maddie held hands and played jumping over the tiny waves.

Tina held out her hand to me. 'Come on, Selma!' she said.

So I wriggled my toes out of my flip-flops and went paddling too. The water was absolutely freezing! And there was all this mucky brown slithery stuff floating in it.

'Yuck! What's *that*?' I squealed.

'It's only seaweed, silly,' said Phil.

'It's horrible,' I said.

'It can't hurt you,' Maddie laughed.

I wasn't so sure. It looked like this huge writhing sea monster ready to get me. Then a great strand wound itself right round my ankles, and I shrieked and ran back onto the beach.

Tina held out her hand to me. She didn't seem a bit scared of the seaweed herself. She was such a funny, wussy little thing, and yet she could be so brave at times. She'd cheerfully pick up the biggest wriggly worm without even shuddering. 'You can splash past the seaweedy part ever so quickly. Come out here with me! The water's all clear and lovely,' she called.

'No, I don't fancy paddling – I might get my new shorts wet. I don't want to spoil them,' I said quickly.

Tina didn't seem to care about getting *her* shorts wet. She jumped about an awful lot and got soaked all the way up to her neck, but she just laughed and laughed.

Her mum got a bit fussed when she saw the state of her, and insisted we all go back to the caravan and towel ourselves down and put on dry clothes. It all seemed a bit mad to me.

'It's what we did last year,' said Tina. 'It's one of our special family things now.'

'Our funny little rituals,' said her dad. 'You're probably thinking we're mad as a box of frogs, Selma.'

They *were* a bit mad. They all spent ages making a sandcastle on the beach. Even my little brother Sam would have thought he was a bit old for messing about with buckets and spades. Still, this was an actual castle with turrets and scraped-out windows and elaborate shell decorations. We dug a moat all

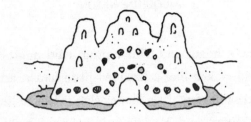

the way round, and then Phil and Maddie and Tina kept dashing into the sea with buckets so they could fill the moat up with water.

I joined in too, but it seemed a bit pointless as the water drained away as fast as they filled it up. And they'd built the sandcastle too near the sea anyway. It would all get washed away when the tide came in.

'Isn't it a waste of all that hard work?' I asked. 'At least when Tina and I made our butterfly garden at school, it stayed put.'

'Good point,' said Tina's dad. 'But somehow it makes it more special. And tell you what – you could take a picture of our castle, Selma, so we can all remember it.'

I took lots of photos of the sandcastle. Then they all lay on their backs in the sand and looked up at the clouds. Tina's dad said he thought one of the clouds looked like a horse's head, and Tina's mum said another cloud looked like a lopsided little house, and Phil said a few little blobby clouds looked like ducklings, and Maddie said no, they looked more like mushrooms, and Tina said a cloud high up in the sky looked like a butterfly. Trust Tina – she's still mad on butterflies. I didn't think the clouds looked like horses' heads or houses or ducklings or mushrooms or even butterflies. They just looked like clouds to me. But I took photos of them all the same. I made Tina sit up so I could take selfies of us with the clouds all round our heads.

'See – doesn't it look funny, as if we've both got bouncy white curls!' I said.

'Let's see,' said Phil.

'Take one of us too,' said Maddie.

'No – I can't keep *on* taking photos. I'll use up all my memory,' I said.

'Let's hope your memory gets used up *soon*,' said Tina's mum.

'How about a game of French cricket now we've all had a little rest?' suggested Tina's dad.

Phil and Maddie and Tina all whooped. Tina saw that I looked uncertain. 'French cricket's ever such fun,' she said. 'You'll love it, Selma.'

I wasn't so sure. I didn't like the sound of it. I didn't know any French and I'd never played cricket, but I'd seen them playing it on one of the sports channels and it looked terribly complicated and dead boring. But it turned out that French cricket really was great fun, and easy-peasy to learn.

I was good at it. Really good. Much better than Maddie, and she's meant to be the sporty one. I really whacked that ball and I didn't drop a single catch. I was even better at bowling. I can throw ferociously. I bowled everyone out, even Tina's dad.

'You're Man of the Match, Selma, without a doubt,' he said, clapping me on the back.

Then we had a barbecue on the beach, and that was even better than French cricket. Tina's dad cooked sausages and chicken drumsticks, and Tina's mum passed round a big plastic

 bowl of salad stuff and chunks of thickly buttered bread. Some of the other families from the caravan site had picnics, but no one else had a proper barbecue. They all looked at us enviously.

Three boys came past, sniffing up the glorious sausage/chicken smell.

'Give us a sausage, mate!' they begged.

'Sorry, lads. Off you go now,' said Tina's mum.

But Tina's dad's an old softie and gave each of them a sausage, even wrapping them in paper napkins so their hands wouldn't get burned.

'Honestly!' said Tina's mum.

'Well, we've got heaps and heaps,' he said sheepishly.

'Yes, but now half the beach is going to come begging,' she tutted.

Almost immediately two older girls wandered up to us, one fair and one dark. They wore bikini tops and little short shorts and they both had their belly buttons pierced.

'Got any more sausages going begging?' the fair one asked, giving Tina's dad a flirty smile.

'What did I say?' said Tina's mum, bristling.

'Sorry, girls,' he said.

'You gave those boys over there a sausage!' said the dark girl.

'Yes, well, I haven't got any more going spare,' said Tina's dad, trying to stand firm.

'Meanie! Look, you've got heaps sizzling on that barbecue!' the fair one said.

'For my family,' said Tina's dad. That gave me a little thrill. I liked him counting me as part of the family.

'You've got seven there!' said the fair girl. 'You could spare one for us. We don't mind sharing.'

'Yes, but two are for me,' he told her.

'Then you're a right old greedy-guts,' said the dark girl.

'Yeah, look at his big fat stomach,' said her friend.

'You shut up!' I said indignantly, furious that she dared criticize such a lovely man.

'That's enough of your lip. Push off now,' he said.

'Yes, go away at once. What a cheek!' Tina's mum was outraged.

They sauntered off very slowly, peering back over their shoulders, pulling faces at us. I pulled a hideous face back. So did Phil and Maddie and Tina.

'Now then, there's no need to copy them. They're silly, rude girls. Just ignore them,' said Tina's mum.

'They're not ignoring us,' I said.

The fair one bent down and picked something up. A pebble.

'Watch out!' I said.

She chucked it at us, but she was a lousy shot. It fell short.

'Stop that!' said Tina's dad.

The dark girl tried too. She had a better aim. Her pebble glanced off the sole of my trainer. It was only a little pebble and it didn't hurt, but I wasn't going to let her get away with that. I picked up my own pebble and threw it. Bull's-eye! It hit her right on her bottom! She squealed and sprinted away, her friend running after her.

'Wow!' said Phil and Maddie and Tina.

But Tina's mum took hold of me, looking furious. 'Selma, you must never, ever throw stones! That's so dangerous. If you'd hit her on the head, you could have hurt her really seriously,' she said.

'But I didn't aim at her head, I got her on the bum!' I said. 'And they both threw stones first. Didn't they?' I said, appealing to Tina's dad.

'Yes, they did, and you were trying to protect us, and that's very sweet of you, but even so, you must never, ever throw stones.'

'Well, what was I supposed to do, then?' I asked.

'Just ignore them. Tina's daddy would have dealt with those silly girls,' said Tina's mum.

'Never! He's too soft,' I said. I didn't mean

to be rude. I *liked* him being soft. I just meant that he was too kind and cheery and gentle to frighten them off. But he looked so hurt, and it made me feel terrible. I didn't really care that Tina's mum didn't like me, but I hated Tina's dad not liking me now.

He didn't tell me off. Even Tina's mum stopped nagging. But they were kind of cool with me after that and I knew I was in disgrace. We stayed on the beach until it got dark, and then Tina's mum took us back to the caravan while Tina's dad cleared up all the barbecue things.

We still had to unpack everything, though my things only took a minute or two. Tina and Phil and Maddie had heaps of stuff to sort out, and Tina's mum had two big suitcases full of clothes to try to squash into one small wardrobe. Then there was a great palaver about washing. Tina and Phil and Maddie all got into their funny babyish pyjamas and washed their hands and faces and cleaned their teeth. It took ages and seemed a total waste of time to me. I just jumped up onto one of the top bunks in my pants.

'Hey, that's *my* bunk,' said Phil, her mouth still frothing with toothpaste.

'Well, I bagged it first,' I said.

'No, it's truly mine. I had that exact same bunk last year,' said Phil.

I sighed, rolling my eyes. 'All right, diddums. Don't get upset.' I jumped down without bothering with the ladder and clambered up onto the opposite bunk.

'No, that's *my* bunk,' said Maddie. 'And we're not allowed to jump down like that. You could really hurt yourself. Mum said.'

'What rubbish,' I said, though actually the soles of my feet were burning and I'd jarred my spine. 'So which is your bunk, Tina?'

'This one,' said Tina, pointing to a bottom bunk. 'But you can have it if you like, Selma. I can sleep on the spare one.'

'Why don't you ever get a turn at a top bunk?' I asked. 'That's not fair.'

'Tina can't go in a top bunk because she's

JACQUELINE WILSON

too little – if she fell out she'd really, really hurt herself because of her poorly heart,' said Phil. 'Mum said.'

'I'm a bit sick of your mum and all the stuff she says,' I told her. Perhaps I said it a bit too loudly, because Tina's mum came bustling in, pink in the face.

'Come on, girls – into bed. Selma, you'll be sleeping in that bottom bunk opposite Tina. Now settle down sensibly. You can read and chat for a few minutes, but then I want you to turn off the light and go to sleep. Night-night now.'

Phil said night-night and got a kiss, though her mum had to stand on tiptoe to reach her. Maddie said night-night and got a kiss, though her mum had to stand on tiptoe to reach her too. Tina said night-night and got a kiss, though this time her mum had to bend down carefully so she didn't bump her head.

I didn't say night-night. I didn't get a kiss. I didn't care one bit.

Then Tina's dad came in, and he did the whole night-night, kiss-kiss routine too.

I kept quiet. Afterwards I thought he'd leave, but he knelt down beside my bunk.

'Night-night, Selma,' he said, and he gave me a quick kiss on my cheek.

'Night,' I said in a tiny voice. I was a bit choked up – I don't know why.

'Sorry we were a bit shirty with you earlier, pet. It's just that it's very dangerous to throw stones,' he whispered. 'Promise you'll never, ever throw stones again, Selma?'

'OK, I promise, but that fair girl threw hers first!'

'I know, I know. I've had a little word with her and her friend. They came back along the beach while I was packing up the barbecue. I told them how silly it was to throw stones too. Then I suggested we all be friends, and invited them to come to a barbecue with us tomorrow,' he said.

'Are they *coming*?'

'I don't think so – but I'm pretty sure we won't have any more trouble with them.'

I wasn't so sure, but I didn't feel like arguing with him now.

Then we had this reading time. Phil and Maddie and Tina took it in turns to read aloud from a silly picture book about three little pigs. I wrinkled my nose and looked sideways at them.

'OK, I know it's babyish, but it's our favourite,' said Phil. 'I do the voice for Peter Pig.'

'We always read it. Have done for ages,' said Maddie. 'I do Percy Pig.'

'And I'm the baby, Pompom Pig. He has this funny little squeaky voice. You can say it with me, Selma,' said Tina.

'No thanks,' I said.

'Oh, go on. You have to join in too. Please. I know it's silly, but it's fun,' she pleaded.

I had to join in because Tina is my best friend for ever and that's what you have to do. But it *wasn't* fun. It was very, very silly. Every time one of the pigs spoke, Phil or Maddie or Tina made these little snorty noises. Then they all laughed, each and every time. The first time I tried to laugh, just to be polite, but I couldn't keep it up. Even my stupid brother Sam wouldn't have found it funny.

I couldn't wait for the story to be over. But after that it got even worse. First of all Phil and Maddie started talking about all the things that had happened last summer. I tried talking to Tina about our butterfly garden – about the planting we could do next year – but I could tell she wasn't really listening. When I was talking, she suddenly giggled and said, 'Do you remember the time Mum fell asleep on the lilo while we were all swimming and the tide came in and her sandals floated away!'

They all spluttered with laughter.

'That's not the slightest bit funny,' I said.

That only made them laugh harder. Nothing is more annoying than being with three girls who've got the giggles when you don't feel remotely amused. I was glad when their mum called from the next room, 'Lights out now, girls. Settle down.'

They turned off the light, but they didn't settle down. They had this whole mad routine, saying goodnight to each other.

'Night-night, Phil. You are brill,' Tina and Maddie chanted.

'Night-night, Maddie. You're a baddie,' Tina and Phil chanted.

'Night-night, Tina. You're a runner bean-a,' Phil and Maddie chanted.

There was a pause.

'Let's make up a night-night for Selma,' said Tina. 'What rhymes with Selma?'

They couldn't think of anything. Tina kept trying, muttering, 'Belma, Celma, Delma, Elma, Felma . . .' without any luck.

'I don't want a silly name,' I said.

I was getting sick to death of all their little rituals. I wished Tina was an only child. It would be such fun with just the two of us in the caravan. I'd have the top bunk and Tina would be safe in the bottom bunk, and we'd

tell our own stories and make up our own
funny rhymes. I felt like the odd one out now,
as if Tina wasn't my best friend any more. She
was a triplet, one of three. I was one all by myself.

I put the pillow over my head and
pretended to go to sleep. When Tina whispered
my name, I didn't answer. She tried again and
then gave up. I felt she could have tried a
bit harder. Soon I heard little snores coming
from Phil's bunk, and Maddie started rootling
round in hers. They really were like little pigs.

I started to wish I was back in my bed at
home. My eyes felt hot, and then suddenly they
were wet. I blotted them hard with my pillow.
I never, ever cried. I was Selma, the
girl who was too tough for tears.
But I didn't feel like big, tough
Selma here, where they wouldn't
even let me chuck a stone at a
girl who'd thrown one at me. They
were all stupid, even Tina.

I reached for my phone and started texting
my mum under the covers.

Can u come and fetch me? Don't like it here.

But what if they'd really gone to Disney-land? And even if they were still at home, how would they fetch me? Jason was banned from driving and the car was all smashed up anyway. And he'd go on and on about it, saying stuff about Tina and her family, making out they'd got fed up with me.

He'd be right. They didn't really want me here. Tina's mum had said so. Phil and Maddie didn't like me – any fool could tell that. Tina's dad was nice to me, but then he was nice to everyone. And Tina? Of course she liked me because she was my best friend – so why didn't she tell her stupid sisters to shut up? Why did we have to be stuck with them all the time? Why couldn't we go off by ourselves and have fun?

By the time I finally got to sleep my pillow was wetter than ever. But when I woke up early the next morning, Tina was gently tickling my neck.

'Shh! The others are all asleep!

I thought we could creep out and go to the beach all by ourselves,' she whispered.

'Oh, wow! Yes!' I said.

It took us two minutes to rush in and out of the toilet and shove on shorts and T-shirts. I put my phone in my pocket, of course. We crept about in an exaggerated manner, pointing to our lips and making shushing noises. It made us get the giggles, so then we had to put our hands over our mouths and noses, though we couldn't stop a few snorty noises escaping.

When we got safely out of the caravan without anyone waking up, it was such a relief we practically exploded. We ran down the path between the neat rows of caravans, shrieking with laughter. I think I shrieked much louder than Tina because I was so happy that she wanted to just be with me. Several curtains twitched as we ran past. One man actually put his head out of the door and hissed, 'Pipe down, you two!' That made us laugh even more, because he looked so funny in his pyjamas, with his hair sticking straight up. I badly wanted to take a photo of him, but I knew it wouldn't be wise.

Right at the end of the row, two girls peered sleepily out of the caravan window. They looked familiar. One was fair. One was dark.

'It's *them*!' I told Tina.

They didn't look friendly, for all Tina's dad's peacemaking. One of them mouthed a very rude word at us.

'Um!' said Tina. 'Come on, Selma, run! I don't like those girls.'

'Neither do I.' I stayed just long enough to mouth the word back at them, and then shot off, pulling Tina along behind me.

We ran out of the gate, down the zigzag path, all the way to the beach. Then we charged across the sand, waving our arms.

'Look, I'm like a butterfly!' said Tina. She peered down at her bright blue T-shirt and denim shorts. 'Hey, I'm an Adonis blue!'

I looked at my new green T-shirt. 'And I'm a green hairstreak!'

We laughed, proud of ourselves for knowing so much about butterflies now.

'Maybe we could make a sand butterfly,' I suggested. 'Just the two of us.'

'Great idea!' said Tina. But then she wrinkled her nose. 'We haven't got any spades with us, though. Shall we go back to the caravan and fetch them?'

'No, we might wake someone up,' I said.

'Mmm. Tell you what, I could *draw* a butterfly,' she said.

She searched around and found an ice-lolly stick, then ran back to the damp sand near the sea, where she crouched down and started drawing a big butterfly shape. I took a photo of her. Then I found a proper twiggy stick.

'Here, draw with this instead, Tina – that way you won't have to bend down so much,' I suggested.

'Thanks!' she said gratefully.

I went on searching for useful things. Then

I found a black pebble with a streak of white down it, rather like an eye. 'Hey, look,' I said, holding it out. 'What's that butterfly that has spots like eyes, one on each wing?'

'A meadow brown,' said Tina, who is the world expert on butterflies. 'Oh, you're so brilliant!' She took the stone and placed it carefully on the top right wing.

I grinned. I loved being called brilliant.

'Find another one to go on the other wing then!' Tina commanded.

I did my best. I offered her several dark pebbles, but she shook her head, saying she didn't think they were a proper match. I even found another black one with a white streak, but Tina still shook her head.

'It's not big enough. The poor butterfly would look all wonky. Can't you find one exactly the same?' she said.

'Why do you have to be so flipping fussy?' I said, but I went searching all over the beach to try and please her.

Then, at long last, I found another black

stone with a white streak that looked exactly the right size, and went haring back to her. She'd made the butterfly body and head out of little round black pebbles and pulled two bits off my twiggy stick to make beautiful antennae.

'Wow! It looks fantastic, Tina,' I said. 'Here – how about this stone?'

I put my new find in her hand.

'Yay!' she cried, and set it in the left wing.

'There, it's perfect. Let's take a photo of it,' I said.

'No, wait. It's still not the right colour,' said Tina. 'It's a meadow *brown*.'

'For goodness' sake, you can't *paint* it!' I protested.

'We just need something to drape round inside the wing. Something brown and sort of ruffly at the edges to make the back wings look curvy,' said Tina thoughtfully. She looked towards the sea. 'Something brown and ruffly like . . . seaweed!'

'No way!' I said. 'If you want seaweed, you're fetching it yourself!'

'Please, Selma. I just need to make a few finishing touches,' she said. 'And you'll be able to scoop up more than me.'

'I'm not touching it,' I insisted.

'Selma, you're not *really* scared of seaweed, are you?' she asked.

'Of course I'm not,' I lied. 'But I'm not your dogsbody. If you want it, you can get it yourself.'

'Meanie!' said Tina.

'How can you say that when I found you a proper stick and sorted through thousands and thousands of pebbles to find the exact right one for Miss Picky Knickers?' I protested.

Tina sighed. 'Yeah, you've got a point. OK, I'll go and get the seaweed.'

It took her four or five trips down to the sea to get enough. By this time she was sounding a bit gaspy. I started to feel worried. I knew she wasn't very strong. I should be helping her, but I couldn't stand the thought of scooping that horrid slimy stuff up with my bare hands.

I was relieved when Tina started draping the seaweed inside her outline, repositioning the eye pebbles on top. She was right: it did look extra specially effective with the lower wings frilly at the edges. In fact, when she was finished, it looked a work of true genius.

'You're the one who's brilliant, Tina. It's even more of a shame it will all be gone when the tide comes in,' I said. 'But I'll record it, OK?'

I took photos of the butterfly from every angle, and then I took more of Tina squatting proudly beside it.

'Let me take one of you with the butterfly. I couldn't have made it without you,' said Tina.

I knelt down beside it, pointing proudly at the pebble eye spots, while Tina faffed around with my phone.

'The other way round, silly!' I said. She might have been a genius at art, but she was useless at anything practical.

She stood up, then crouched down, trying to get me and the sand butterfly into focus. She climbed onto a little rock so that she was at the right height. And then I saw two girls suddenly jumping up onto the rock beside her. One fair, one dark. With menacing looks.

'Watch out, Tina!' I cried.

She swung round, one hand up, holding my phone.

'You giving it to me?' the fair girl said, trying to snatch it. 'Thanks!'

Tina held onto my phone valiantly, but the dark girl gave her a push. It wasn't much of a push, but Tina's little and she fell off the rock onto the sand.

'How dare you!' I screamed, and seized an eye-spot pebble.

Promise you'll never, ever throw stones again, Selma!

It was a big stone. It could do a lot of

damage . . . but I *had* to defend Tina. There was no other way. I had to break my promise. Unless . . .

The two girls were running now. I took a deep breath, scooped up two huge handfuls of disgusting slimy seaweed from the butterfly's wings, ran after them and took aim.

Splodge! I got the fair girl right on the head.

I threw another lump. I missed the dark girl's head, but the sea-weed slithered all down her back.

They shrieked and shuddered wonderfully.

'Amazing!' gasped Tina, picking herself up. 'And I've still got your phone safe. I didn't get it sandy – look!'

'Give it here a second,' I said.

I switched it to video and captured the girls sobbing and screaming, still covered in seaweed.

'There! I've recorded you two, and if you don't leave us alone now, I'll put it on YouTube and I bet it will go viral and you'll both end up laughing stocks!' I said. 'You can't get the better of me. I'm Selma, and I'm the meanest girl ever, and everyone's scared of me!'

'Except me,' said Tina.

The girls turned and ran off!

'Oh, wow, Selma, they really *are* scared now,' Tina laughed.

'They make out they're so tough, but they're total wimps, scared of a few bits of seaweed!' I said, though I was busy burying my hands in the soft sand further up the beach, desperate to get rid of that horrible slimy, slippery feel.

Tina was looking sadly at her butterfly. 'It's a shame it's spoiled now, without its brown wings,' she said. 'Shall we make it again?'

I looked at the time on my phone. 'Actually, I think we'd better get back. Won't your mum and dad be up by now?'

'OK. But let's sneak out again early tomorrow and make another butterfly,' said Tina. 'Just you and me.'

So we did. I even fetched some seaweed myself, though I did use Tina's mum's Marigold gloves.

She got a bit narked when she found out. Still, for the rest of the holiday she didn't nag me too much. And Tina's dad was lovely to me.

'Strange how those girls didn't come round for our barbecue, though,' he said. 'They seem to be keeping well away. Still, it shows that talking things through nearly always stops people doing silly things.'

'Nearly always,' I agreed, and Tina winked at me.

We didn't tell Tina's dad or mum about the seaweed incident, of course. But Tina told Phil and Maddie, and I showed them my video clip. We all laughed and laughed. Phil and Maddie aren't too bad, actually. Sometimes it was fun, all of us playing together.

But the best parts of all were when it was just Tina and me.

*In which Pea has just moved to a
new house, and is looking for a friend . . .*

PEA STEPPED GINGERLY around the porridge, and peered out of the window.

The other side of their half-a-house had a garden like the twin of their own, except with neat grass, a climbing frame with monkey bars, and a vegetable patch instead of lumpy paving and a shed. You could see over the wall between the two quite clearly from Clover's orange-and-silver bedroom. And in the garden, beside the faded red-and-blue football, was a person sitting on the grass reading a book. It looked about Pea's age, the person. It had floppy brown hair, and she couldn't tell if it was a boy or a girl.

Pea waved her arm, and knocked on the window.

The person looked up, scanning the sky with a frown. Then the person – it really was impossible to tell if it was a girl or a boy – saw her, smiled widely, and waved too: a proper, excited, pleased-to-meet-you sort of wave.

That was definitely FRIENDLY.

Pea spun about, knocked the porridge bowl so that it splattered up Clover's ankles, hissed 'Sorry!' to her, and hurried back down to the garden.

But it was starting to rain, and though she called 'Hello?' there was no answer. By the time she'd raced back upstairs to Clover's room (where she was not at all welcome), the next-door garden was empty, and fat raindrops were splashing against the windowpane.

All the same, Pea was thrilled. There was a potential new Dot next door, *and* it had been reading. Pea mentally ticked off 'Imaginative (likes books)' on her 'Best Friend Requirements' list at once.

The next day there was a large sign on Clover's bedroom door, with

Clover's Private Bedroom
Knocking Required

in scrolly writing on it. Pea was only allowed in to hover hopefully at Clover's window as long as she agreed to let Clover paint a stinky yellow mixture onto her head.

'Apparently, the very best thing for hair is a sort of apricot that only grows in India,' Clover said, wiping off a dribble that was running down Pea's neck. 'But the astringent qualities of vinegar and conditioning proper- ties of egg yolks are a good substitute. It said so in my leaflet.'

'Mmm,' said Pea, holding her nose, and noting that Clover hadn't put any eggs or vinegar on her *own* hair.

By the time the person arrived in the

garden, Pea's head had dried hard and shiny, like a shell.

Pea waved frantically – but the floppy-haired person didn't even look up. She or he half-heartedly kicked the tatty red-and-blue football around, looking bored.

'You can't go outside like that!' said Clover, rapping on Pea's shiny eggy head as she tried to run out to the garden to shout over the wall.

It took for ever to wash all the egg out, and by the time Pea's hair was clean(ish), the floppy-haired person had gone.

The next day, when Pea sneaked into Clover's room to wait, and then to frantically wave (Clover was in the bath, doing something with orange peel), the person gave her a severe and ominous glare, then went straight back indoors.

It was very confusing.

'It might be a prisoner being held against their will,' said Tinkerbell darkly. 'They could be being hideously tortured for most of the day, and only be allowed out every now and then, for good behaviour. And if anyone sees them waving, back indoors they go for more thumbscrews.'

Pea took this very seriously. She hadn't really believed that Dot had been a secret spy in need of rescue, but this was different: there was definitely something odd going on next door. There was a sign on the red-brick pillar at the end of the drive: a square brass plate, with DR KARA SKIDELSKY & DR G. M. F. PAGET: CHILD PSYCHOLOGY & FAMILY THERAPY etched into the metal. Different people scrunched up the gravelly drive every day – always children, usually with an adult or two to drop them off or pick them up. They always looked worried. Sometimes they were crying. Pea suspected that Dr Kara Skidelsky or Dr G. M. F. Paget was quite capable of keeping one of them behind, for imprisoning purposes.

She began to imagine chains and padlocks, just on the other side of the wall, and resolved to learn semaphore *and* Morse code in case the waving was really a desperate signal for help. Tinkerbell made flags, and they stood at opposite ends of the landing, trying to spell each other's names. Tinkerbell definitely seemed happier, now there was plotting to do to take her mind off Tenby – and Pea remembered that her little sister could be quite kind sometimes, even if her eyes did light up alarmingly whenever she said 'thumbscrews'. But it turned out that semaphore was quite complicated and boring to learn, and there was a very good reason someone had invented text messages instead. Unfortunately, imprisoned persons didn't tend to have mobile phones – and neither did Pea or Tinkerbell.

That afternoon Clover put up a new sign:

Clover's Private Bedroom
No Entry at All to People under 14,
Not Even if You Knock.
GO AWAY!

Banished, they holed up in Tinkerbell's bedroom – Tinkerbell standing on her bed, ear pressed up against the mysterious nailed-up door; Pea kneeling to peer under the bed at that telltale crack of light. There was a piano being played somewhere in the neighbouring house, and the music – the *Moonlight Sonata*, very slow, with the same part being played over and over, always going wrong at the same place – drifted eerily through the wall. They couldn't hear any rattling chains or screams of terror, but the stop-start piano was quite creepy enough.

'We could try un-nailing this door,' said Tinkerbell, poking under a nail with her finger-tip. 'That must go straight into the house next door.'

'Tink, you mustn't, ever!' said Pea, appalled. 'That would be like breaking into their house!'

That wasn't the whole reason. Pea had read *Coraline* last year, and though she knew it was only a story, it seemed best for everyone if the door between the houses stayed nailed shut. Just in case.

There had to be another way of getting a message to the person next door.

When the tatty red-and-blue football bounced into their garden again a few days later, Pea had a brainwave.

ARE YOU A PRISONER?
IF YOU NEED RESCUING, PUT REPLY INSIDE
FOOTBALL AND THROW IT OVER OUR WALL.
love from Pea (the girl next door)
★

She tucked the note through a small hole in the stitching of the football, and got Tinkerbell to kick it high up in the air, back over the wall.

Then Pea and Tinkerbell knocked on Clover's door, again and again, until it was obvious that *not* letting them in would be much more annoying.

'We have to check something – it's very important,' said Tinkerbell, marching past Clover.

The person was in the garden, idly kicking the red-and-blue football against their wall – so it had definitely found its way into the right garden. But after a while – without a glance up at the window – she or he went inside.

'Maybe they'll notice there's a note inside later?' said Tinkerbell, not sounding convinced.

'What if the horrible imprisoning doctors find it first?' said Pea.

'What?' said Clover, who was reclining on her bed with cucumber slices over her eyes.

Tinkerbell explained their fears for the poor chained-up, thumbscrewed person.

'Are you two mental?' said Clover. 'The person next door isn't horribly imprisoned. They've got a piano. There are monkey bars in their garden. And look – now they're eating an ice cream.'

Pea watched miserably as the person returned to the garden, licking a vanilla cone.

It was comforting to think no one was being chained to a wall and thumbscrewed, but now there was no reason at all for the friendly waving to have stopped. Unless, with all those other children coming and going, they simply didn't have time for more friends.

The floppy-haired person probably had a million Dots of his or her own already; no need for a Pea.

Pea sat dejectedly on Clover's bed.

'Did you really want to be friends with this next-door person?' asked Clover, quite gently and ever so slightly Mumlike.

Pea nodded.

'We tried learning semaphore and everything,' said Tinkerbell.

'Then you can't just give up,' said Clover. 'They've got that piano next door. I could go round to ask if I can practise on it – say once

a week – and you could come too, and accidentally bump into her. Or him. Whichever it is.'

Pea felt much better now that someone
else was in charge of finding her a best friend
for a bit.

Clover waited until quarter past two on a
Monday afternoon ('because anyone who's at
home at quarter past two on a Monday will
probably like being distracted by the doorbell
– Mum always does'), and scrunched down the
gravelly path.

Pea and Tinkerbell waited at the end
of the drive, by the red-brick pillar with the
engraved brass plate for DR KARA SKIDELSKY &
DR G. M. F. PAGET: CHILD PSYCHOLOGY & FAMILY
THERAPY. Even without any imprisoning
going on beyond it, Pea still found it quite
intimidating, for a brass square was almost
certainly more important than a blue plaque.

When the front door swung open, they
dipped behind the pillar.

Pea could hear Clover's voice, unusually
meek, then another, rather brisk, in reply,

and couldn't resist peering out. The person on the doorstep was a pale, elongated lady: long skirt, long cardigan, long strings of beads. Clover looked oddly pink and three-dimensional beside her. They talked quietly for a short time. It all looked very business-like. They even shook hands.

Then the front door closed, and Clover hurried down the path.

'That was Dr G. M. F. Paget, and the G stands for Genevieve,' Clover told them, once they were safely back inside their own front door. 'She wasn't *very* scary. But she said she was with a patient, and actually quarter past two isn't at all a good time to ring people's doorbells. We should tell Mum she's doing afternoons all wrong. *Anyway*, she said I can play their piano whenever I like! *And* she finishes early on Tuesdays and we can come for afternoon tea tomorrow. All of us. She said she's been meaning to invite us over ever since we moved in. *And*' – Clover beamed at Pea – 'she asked me to give this to "the red-headed girl from the window".'

Clover pressed a folded scrap of paper into Pea's hand.

Dear Pea (it said),
Thank you for the note (I think
it was for me). I am not a prisoner
but I am quite bored. Come and visit.
We have monkey bars.
From Sam

Pea glowed. Her person had a name (a frustrating one, true; if only they were called something helpful like Jack or Julietta), and the waving had been friendly all along, and they hadn't thought she was silly for writing 'love from Pea' on her note or thinking they might be horribly imprisoned.

And tomorrow she would meet them properly, for afternoon tea.

We hope you enjoyed reading
BUTTERFLY BEACH

Here's a selection of some of Jacqueline Wilson's
other brilliant stories – which one will
you read next?

THE BUTTERFLY CLUB

Tina can no longer hide
behind her triplet sisters as
she's teamed up with tough
Selma for the first time . . .

Sisters also star in . . .

THE WORST THING
ABOUT MY SISTER

Can tomboy Marty and
her girly sister Melissa
ever get along?

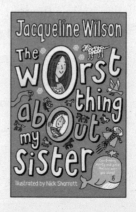

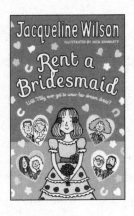

*Marty pops up
again in . . .*

RENT A BRIDESMAID

Tilly's new friends
help make her bridesmaid
dreams come true . . .

*From new friends to
lifelong pals . . .*

BEST FRIENDS

Gemma and Alice are inseparable
– until Alice moves to Scotland!
Gemma hopes Alice won't
forget her . . .

*From faraway friends to a
mum who can't be reached . . .*

THE LONGEST
WHALE SONG

Can Ella's love bring
Mum back?

VISIT JACQUELINE'S FANTASTIC WEBSITE!

There's a whole Jacqueline Wilson town
to explore! You can generate your own
special username, customize your online
bedroom, test your knowledge of Jacqueline's
books with fun quizzes and puzzles, and
upload book reviews. There's lots of fun stuff
to discover, including competitions, book
trailers and Jacqueline's scrapbook.
And if you love writing, visit the special
storytelling area!

Plus, you can hear the latest news from
Jacqueline in her monthly diary, find out
whether she's doing events near you, read
her fan-mail replies, and chat to other fans
on the message boards!

  www.jacquelinewilson.co.uk

HAPPY BIRTHDAY WORLD BOOK DAY!

Let's celebrate . . .

Can you believe this year is our **20th birthday** – and thanks
to you, as well as our amazing authors, illustrators, booksellers,
librarians and teachers, there's SO much to celebrate!

Did you know that since WORLD BOOK DAY began in 1997,
we've given away over **275 million book tokens**? WOW! We're
delighted to have brought so many books directly into the hands of
millions of children and young people just like you, with a gigantic
assortment of fun activities and events and resources and quizzes
and dressing-up and games too – we've even broken a **Guinness
World Record**!

Whether you love discovering books that make you **laugh**, CRY,
hide under the covers or **drive your imagination wild**,
with WORLD BOOK DAY, there's always something for everyone to
choose–as well as ideas for exciting new books to try at bookshops,
libraries and schools everywhere.

And as a small charity, we couldn't do it without a lot of help from
our friends in the publishing industry and our brilliant sponsor,
NATIONAL BOOK TOKENS. Hip-hip hooray to them and three
cheers to you, our readers and everyone else who has joined us over
the last 20 years to make WORLD BOOK DAY happen.

Happy Birthday to us – and happy reading to you!

Illustrations © Liz Pichon

#WorldBookDay20

BOOK IN
FOR YOUR NEW ADVENTURE TODAY

CELEBRATING

WORLD
BOOK
DAY

20
2 MARCH 2017

3 brilliant ways to continue YOUR reading adventure

1 VISIT YOUR LOCAL BOOKSHOP

Your go-to destination for awesome reading recommendations and events with your favourite authors and illustrators.

 Booksellers.org.uk/ bookshopsearch

2 JOIN YOUR LOCAL LIBRARY

Browse and borrow from a huge selection of books, get expert ideas of what to read next, and take part in wonderful family reading activities – all for FREE!

 Findalibrary.co.uk

3 DISCOVER A WORLD OF STORIES ONLINE

32 podcasts to try

Stuck for ideas of what to read next? Plug yourself in to our brilliant new podcast library! Sample a world of amazing books, brought to life by amazing storytellers. **worldbookday.com**